"Phil, Phil," said
Stephanie Gopher.
"Can you hear me?"

Phil Elephant was slowly swaying back and forth. His eyes were shut.

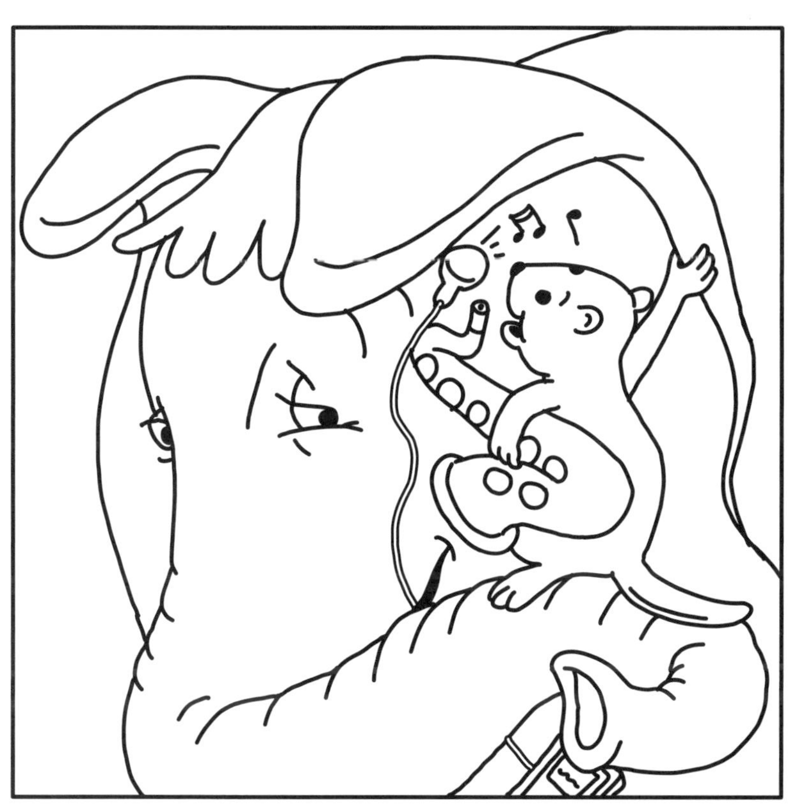

Stephanie jumped up on his trunk. She lifted his huge ear and yelled into it.

"Phil, Phil," she said. "Can you hear me now?"

"What?" asked Phil.
"I can't hear a thing.
Wait. Let me take off
my earphones."

Phil took off his
earphones.
"Now I am all ears,
Stephanie," said Phil,
with a smile.

"I was lost in the
sounds of my music,"
said Phil. "What's up?"

"I want to play something for you," Stephanie said to her friend. "I made up a tune on my saxophone."
"Play it, Stephanie," said Phil.

Stephanie Gopher jumped
down to the ground.
She stood up in her best
performing pose. Her
saxophone gleamed in
the sun.

Phil leaned on a tree
and waited.
"It goes like this,"
she said, as she took
a deep breath and
began to play.

Her notes had the shine
of sun and the buzz of
bees. They rang like bells
and swelled like the seas.

Phil stretched his ears
wide to take in all
the notes.
Stephanie Gopher played
hard and kept time with
a tap of her foot.

As Stephanie played
each phrase, Phil felt
like he was floating.
He just had to be a part
of this joyful sound!

Phil lifted his trunk high
and began to trumpet.
"Rooty-toot-toot" came
the sounds from his trunk.

Stephanie and Phil were
so lost in the music that
they did not see the crowd
Sophie Snake was twisting
and twirling.

Ralph the Bird was
floating and swirling.
Joseph was rocking
and jumping.

Huge Humphrey
joined the gang, too.
It was a sight to see!